The Betraye

Vikram Sathi

www.draft2digital.com

Copyright

Published by: Education Corner

Draft2digital Edition

Table of Contents

Preface

Within the pages of "The Betrayer," an enchanting novella, lies a tale that will take you on an emotional odyssey. As you embark on this literary journey, prepare to be captivated by the intertwining threads of love, loss, and redemption that weave a mesmerizing tapestry of human experiences.

In the world of this novella, the characters come alive, each carrying their own burdens and secrets. Their lives intersect and diverge, revealing the delicate intricacies of relationships and the profound impact of choices made in the name of love.

It is a story that delves into the depths of human emotions, where happiness and heartache coexist, and the lines between trust and betrayal blur.

Through the eyes of our protagonist, Anand, you will witness the complexities of societal expectations, the struggles against caste boundaries, and the tender vulnerabilities that arise when love is tested.

Alongside Anand, you will navigate a labyrinth of emotions, contemplating the power of forgiveness, the resilience of the human spirit, and the pursuit of redemption.

"The Betrayer" invites you to contemplate the universal themes of human connection and the consequences that unfold when trust is shattered.

It is a tale that will resonate with anyone who has experienced the elation and pain that love can bring, offering insights into the intricacies of relationships and the fragile nature of the human heart.

As you immerse yourself in the pages of "The Betrayer," allow yourself to be swept away by its evocative storytelling and richly drawn characters.

Engage in introspection as you explore the themes of identity, societal expectations, and the search for true meaning in a world teeming with contradictions.

This novella is a tribute to the power of words, the enduring capacity of stories to touch our souls, and the empathy they foster within us. It is an invitation to ponder the complexities of the human experience and to reflect upon our own choices, joys, and regrets.

So, dear reader, I invite you to turn the page and embark on this transformative journey. Traverse the emotional landscape of "The Betrayer," where love and betrayal dance a delicate tango.

Allow yourself to be captivated by the characters' struggles and triumphs, and discover within their stories the echoes of your own hopes, dreams, and desires.

May the words within these pages resonate deeply within your heart, igniting a flame of contemplation, and reminding you of the timeless power of storytelling!

All the Best

Chapter 1

My Old Friend

I arrived at Preetam's abode, my heart brimming with anticipation as I prepared to reunite with him after a long and arduous year apart. With a mixture of eagerness and trepidation, I pressed the doorbell, my impatience echoing in the stillness of the air.

After what felt like an eternity, the door creaked open, revealing a sight that momentarily shattered my expectations. Preetam, once vibrant and full of life, stood before me, his haggard appearance overshadowing his familiar features.

The absence of his lustrous hair, his frail frame, and the undeniable aura of illness that surrounded him momentarily deceived me into believing that I had encountered a stranger.

"Dude, what has befallen you?" I inquired, my voice tinged with genuine concern.

"First, come inside," Preetam beckoned, his voice feeble yet retaining its warmth, as he ushered me into the confines of his home, promptly closing the door behind us.

As I surveyed the transformed surroundings of his abode, a profound sense of change washed over me. Preetam's once cluttered shelves, once adorned with an array of alcohol bottles, now stood adorned with a diverse collection of books.

The metamorphosis was striking, reflecting a newfound sense of refinement and intellectual pursuit that had permeated his life. Before I could articulate my curiosity, Preetam, in his weakened state, retreated to the kitchen, intent on retrieving something meaningful.

As I settled onto the inviting embrace of the sofa, my eyes roamed the nearby table and discovered a familiar sight: an album capturing the bittersweet essence of our farewell party.

My fingers delicately flipped through the pages, revealing a collage of memories frozen in time. Among the jubilant snapshots of Preetam dancing with various enchanting companions, one particular photograph seized my attention—a moment frozen forever—

depicting Preetam enveloped in a heartfelt embrace with Neelima.

The image acted as a key, unlocking a floodgate of reminiscences that transported me back to those bygone days, evoking a wave of emotions.

"Twenty-four, she is my 24th girlfriend!" Preetam declared, a blend of weariness and a hint of pride coloring his words, as he lifted his glass in a cheerful salute.

"Cheers!" I reciprocated, my voice resonating with warmth, yet quickly seizing the moment. "Hold on, my friend. What do you have there, in your hand?"

Preetam's eyes twinkled mischievously as he replied, "Ah, it's just coke, my dear pal.

You know I don't partake in alcoholic beverages."

Asserting my preference with a soothing tone, I countered, "But this is our farewell party, Preetam. You know I refrain from drinking."

Undeterred, he extended a generous offer, his voice filled with camaraderie, "Come on, just a sip or two to mark this memorable occasion?"

"Apologies, my friend, but I'll have to decline," I replied politely, steadfast in my decision not to indulge. "Now, tell me, who is this new flame of yours? Could she possibly be your fifth girlfriend, excluding the exes?"

Preetam chuckled, the sound laced with a hint of affectionate exasperation. "Ah, you never forget to remind me of my past romantic escapades. Perhaps you should consider becoming my personal assistant."

Taking another sip, Preetam leaned in, his voice hushed. "By the way, her name is Neelima. You're familiar with her, right?"

A surge of recognition washed over me. "Ah, yes, Neelima. She's the close friend of Chandani, if I recall correctly. And if I'm not mistaken, Chandani happens to be one of your previous girlfriends. So, Neelima must have an intimate understanding of the ins and outs of your romantic entanglements, doesn't she?"

I paused, letting the question hang in the air, curious to know Preetam's response.

"And then?" I pressed, intrigued by Preetam's revelation. "How did she come to accept your proposal?"

Preetam burst into laughter, a mixture of surprise and amusement on his face. "You won't believe it, my friend, but the girl who proposed to me was Neelima! It seems like the tables had turned. But you know what? In the grand scheme of things, such details hardly matter. Love operates in mysterious ways. And let me tell you, Neelima didn't propose to me out of genuine affection. It was more because she had heard favorable things about me through Chandani—rumors of wealth and lavish spending on girlfriends, among other things. That's what motivated her to make the move. It's all a part of this intricate game called the 'Game of Love,' which you can never fully comprehend," Preetam declared, his words colored by the influence of the alcohol coursing through his veins.

I finished my coke, a sense of disappointment lingering in the air. "I suppose I will never comprehend your version of the 'game' you call love. However, I refuse to accept that as a genuine representation of what love truly is. Love transcends such shallow pursuits. You have no inkling of the depths and complexities that love encompasses," I stated firmly.

Preetam's intoxicated ramblings continued, each word laced with cynicism. "'Love,' as you call it, is only a brand, a commodity, a business thing. It's a label used to sell cheap and inferior products. People are drawn to these subpar offerings but are too ashamed to admit it, so they seek the illusion of a reputable brand—'Love.' You speak of true love as if it were a mere fabrication, existing only in the realms of stories and movies. Directors and writers capitalize on such illusions, creating fantasies that don't truly exist, much like superheroes and aliens. And yet, there are fools like you who fervently believe in the existence of love, just as children believe in superheroes."

His alcohol-fueled words resonated, laden with bitterness and disillusionment, challenging the very notion I held dear.

"Alright, let's go. But before we leave, say goodbye to your new girlfriend," I said, gently taking hold of Preetam's car keys, prepared to drive him back home safely.

After a short while, Preetam returned, his determination heightened. "Man, I'm in the mood to drive. Give me the keys," he insisted.

"Dude, you're clearly intoxicated. It wouldn't be safe for you to drive. Please let me drive," I requested, taking the driver's seat.

Preetam shrugged off my concern, emphasizing his carefree state. "You are a coward, man! Are you scared of the traffic police? Even if we get caught, the bribe we'd have to pay would be less than what I've spent on a single drink," he remarked, nonchalantly fastening his seat belt.

Recognizing the potential risks, I maintained my stance, ensuring our well-being. "Preetam, you're drunk. It's important to prioritize safety. Let me handle the driving," I firmly stated, securing my own seat belt, ready to take control of the situation.

Despite my insistence that I take the wheel, Preetam stubbornly disregarded my concern and pressed down on the accelerator, propelling the car forward.

His judgment clouded by the effects of alcohol, he seemed oblivious to the potential dangers that lay ahead. Worried for our safety, I braced myself, clinging to the seat as the car surged forward.

It became increasingly evident that persuading him to let me drive had proven futile, and now our fate rested in the hands of his impaired decision-making.

Chapter 2

Beggar Woman

As the traffic signal forced us to halt, Preetam continued his enthusiastic participation in the melodious chorus emanating from the FM radio.

Lost in the rhythm, his voice harmonized with the song, oblivious to the world around us. It was in that moment that a gentle knock on my side window startled me.

Turning my attention towards the sound, I discovered a woman, her appearance resembling that of a classic beggar, standing before me with a child in tow.

The child, frail and clothed in tattered garments, bore the undeniable marks of hardship—a trace of dried tears etched upon his cheek. Moved by their plight, I decided to open the window, inviting the woman to speak.

Her voice trembled as she implored me, her words carrying the weight of desperation, "Sir, please spare some money to feed my child. He is weak, and we have no means to sustain ourselves."

Touched by their plight, I reached into my wallet and retrieved a sum of 100 rupees. With compassion, I handed it to the woman, hoping it would bring some relief to their difficult circumstances.

With gratitude overflowing in her eyes, she blessed me and walked away, their presence a poignant reminder of the struggles faced by those less fortunate.

Turning towards Preetam, a mixture of conviction and disbelief etched on my face, I declared, "Dude, you claimed that true love doesn't exist. But look, I just witnessed a glimpse of it. I gave money to that beggar, and she will now feed her hungry child."

I gestured towards the woman who was making her way towards a nearby bakery, her child eagerly pleading for a cake.

As we observed, she abruptly left the child behind and entered a nearby bar, purchasing a drink for herself while the child remained in tears, longing for a simple treat.

Shock washed over me, a stark reminder that my faith had been misplaced. In that moment, I turned to face Preetam, seeking his reaction.

A knowing smile graced Preetam's lips, an acknowledgement of the complexities that exist within human nature.

Simultaneously, I took hold of the steering wheel, mindful of the growing chorus of horns from the vehicles behind us.

Recognizing the urgency, I set the car into motion, our brief encounter with the beggar and her child lingering in my thoughts, challenging my preconceived notions of love and reminding me of the intricacies and contradictions inherent in the human experience.

"Goodnight, buddy," I bid Preetam farewell as I escorted him safely into his home. Parking the car in front of his house, I made my way on foot towards my own residence, situated just a mere hundred meters away. The cool night air embraced me, and as I walked, I couldn't help but reflect on the events of the evening.

The encounter with the beggar and her child had left an indelible mark, challenging my perspectives and igniting a sense of empathy within me.

Despite the uncertainties and complexities of life, I was grateful for moments like these that reminded me of the importance of compassion and understanding in our shared journey.

Exhausted and hungry, I climbed into bed without partaking in a meal. My thoughts were consumed by Preetam, a friend I had known since our college days. I pondered his circumstances, the challenges he faced as a loner in life.

His mother, a divorcee, had bravely left her husband due to his numerous affairs with colleagues.

She single-handedly raised Preetam, but tragically, she passed away three years ago, her life cut short by liver failure, the result of her own battles with alcohol. It was a painful reminder of the demons that haunted their lives.

Despite inheriting his mother's company, a venture that offered him comfort and a life of luxury, Preetam remained aloof, detached from the concept of love. For him, love had been reduced to a mere game, a notion he had vocalized earlier.

His experiences and upbringing seemed to have shaped his cynical perspective, guarding him against the vulnerability that love often entailed. As sleep gradually overcame me, I couldn't help but wonder about the true depths of his emotions, hidden beneath his façade of indifference.

As for myself, I grew up in the same city, surrounded by the echoes of my parents' tumultuous relationship. While they showered me with love and affection, their own bond lacked the depth and connection that true love encompasses.

Theirs was an arranged marriage, a union dictated by societal expectations of caste and sub caste compatibility.

Witnessing their constant quarrels, sometimes over trivial matters and other times seemingly without any reason, left a lasting impression on me.

Observing their turbulent dynamic, my expectations for a future partner were shaped by a deep longing for love and affection. I yearned for a relationship built on genuine emotional connection, believing that love, above all else, should be the foundation upon which two individuals build a life together.

Perhaps it was an inherent desire to compensate for the void I had witnessed in my parents' marriage, but my hopes were anchored in the belief that a profound and unconditional love would permeate every aspect of my own romantic journey.

As my phone emitted a familiar beep, signaling an incoming notification, I instinctively reached for it. To my delight, I discovered that Avantika was online. Avantika, a Facebook friend of mine, held a unique place in my life. Generally, I was not one to engage in conversations with girls, but Avantika was an exception.

Our connection had originated on my birthday when she sent me a friend request accompanied by a playful message: "If you're dissatisfied with your birthday gifts, feel free to reject this request." Intrigued by her lighthearted approach, I accepted her invitation, and thus our virtual bond began.

Over time, Avantika became an active participant in my online activities. She would often comment on my status updates, offering advice and lending a sympathetic ear to my problems.

It was as if she had taken it upon herself to guide me through life's challenges, her comments serving as a beacon of support and understanding.

Avantika's presence had gradually become a comforting presence in my online world, providing a glimpse of the connection I had yearned for—a connection that transcended superficiality and touched upon the depths of genuine human connection.

Chapter 3

Proposal

In the midst of navigating the complexities of life and love, a significant moment arose when a girl named Preeti mustered the courage to propose to me on our college campus.

Uncertain about how to handle the situation, I confided in Preetam, who offered a simple yet definitive response—to accept her proposal. However, my heart remained uncertain, and I longed for someone with whom I could confide in depth.

That night, as if guided by fate, I found Avantika online and greeted her with a simple

"Hi." To my pleasant surprise, our conversation flowed effortlessly, and I soon discovered that she mirrored my own demeanor—thoughtful, sensible, and matured, akin to an old friend.

In the comfort of our virtual exchange, I disclosed the matter of Preeti's proposal, seeking guidance and understanding. Avantika, with her innate wisdom, offered the advice I had secretly hoped for, reassuring me in a way only a kindred spirit could.

In her presence, I found solace and clarity, grateful to have stumbled upon a connection that transcended the boundaries of cyberspace and brought forth a profound sense of companionship and trust.

Avantika's words resonated deeply within me as she cautioned against hasty conclusions, emphasizing the importance of understanding Preeti's true feelings before proceeding further.

She advised against directly asking Preeti about her emotions, as such a direct question might elicit a response influenced by societal expectations rather than genuine affection.

Instead, Avantika suggested that I buy some time, expressing that I would provide a response on another day. This approach would test the authenticity of Preeti's feelings, as true love would withstand the test of patience and wait.

Taking Avantika's advice to heart, I shared this perspective with Preeti the following day.

To my surprise and relief, Preeti responded with unwavering determination, expressing her willingness to wait. She assured me that if she had already waited this long, she could wait a few more days for my answer.

Her unwavering patience hinted at a depth of devotion that transcended mere infatuation, inspiring a glimmer of hope within me.

In that moment, a delicate dance of emotions unfolded, as Avantika's sage counsel had not only guided me through the labyrinth of uncertainty but had also set in motion a series of events that would test the sincerity of the connection between Preeti and me.

The following day, I once again encountered Avantika's online presence. This time, I poured my heart out, sharing every intricate detail of Preetam's intricate love life, the encounter with the beggar woman and her child, and Preetam's jaded perspective on love.

I laid bare the doubts and uncertainties that plagued my mind, seeking solace and guidance in her words.

Avantika's response, laced with unwavering conviction, resonated deeply within me. She affirmed her belief in the existence of love, assuring me that both Preetam and I would come to understand its profound essence in due course.

Her words carried a weight of wisdom, evoking a sense of anticipation and curiosity within me.

In her steadfast belief, I found a glimmer of hope that love, in its truest form, had the power to transcend the disillusionment and skepticism that had clouded Preetam's perception.

As our conversation unfolded, I couldn't help but sense the profound connection we shared, a connection that extended beyond the boundaries of mere acquaintanceship.

Avantika's understanding and empathetic presence ignited a spark within me, kindling a newfound belief in the transformative power of love and the possibilities that lay ahead.

Chapter 4

A Tinge of Regret

As the days continued to slip by, Preetam reveled in the bliss of his newfound romance, while Preeti remained patiently awaiting my response. Meanwhile, a stroke of fortune came my way in the form of a job offer from another city.

It was an opportunity that promised financial stability, albeit at the cost of leaving behind my family, friends, and the city I had called home for so long.

Despite the bittersweet nature of the decision, I ultimately accepted the job, driven by the allure of a promising career path.

In the initial phase, I found solace and contentment in my new job and the unfamiliar surroundings.

The thrill of novelty masked the pangs of homesickness, and I immersed myself in the tasks at hand. However, as time wore on, a sense of longing began to pervade my being, and the absence of my loved ones became an ache I could no longer ignore.

Regrettably, amidst the whirlwind of change and adjustment, I unintentionally neglected Avantika.

Despite noticing her online presence on numerous occasions, I failed to reach out and engage in the meaningful conversations that had once provided solace and understanding.

The demands of my new life and the weight of missing my dear ones had caused me to inadvertently neglect a connection that had held great significance in my heart.

As the realization of my oversight dawned upon me, a tinge of regret washed over my spirit. I yearned to reconnect with Avantika, to once again experience the warmth and depth of our conversations.

Little did I know that the universe had its own plans in store, waiting to unfold the next chapter of our intertwined journeys.

In the midst of my solitude and the weight of longing, Avantika's virtual presence eluded me. Days turned into weeks, and the ache of loneliness gnawed at my soul.

Each phone call to my family became an emotional outpouring, as tears streamed down my face, longing for their comforting embrace.

Then, on one fateful day, I discovered a letter resting delicately on my office desk, accompanied by a single flower. Its words struck a chord deep within me: "How much longer must I wait? I can survive without your response, but I cannot bear to go on without seeing you. Turn around." Intrigued and filled with a mixture of trepidation and hope, I turned around to face the source of the note.

To my astonishment, there stood Preeti, occupying the desk next to mine. She had embarked on a new chapter in her own journey, joining our company.

In that very moment, my mind ceased to wander, consumed by a rush of overwhelming emotions. Without a second thought, I instinctively embraced her, tears of joy mingling with tears of relief.

The entire office bore witness to our embrace, a testament to the love that had blossomed between us.

In that transformative instant, I realized the true meaning of love. It was not a mere game or an illusion; it was a profound connection that transcended time and distance.

Preeti's presence in my life brought an immense sense of fulfillment, surpassing all expectations I had held for love.

Finally, in her arms, I discovered the purest and most genuine form of affection that had eluded me for so long.

With renewed hope and a heart brimming with love, I embarked on a new chapter of my life, hand-in-hand with Preeti, cherishing the beauty of our shared journey and the indomitable power of true love.

In the present moment, as I examined the photograph before me, a sense of intrigue and curiosity stirred within. Unlike the other pictures, this particular image held a distinct quality.

Neelima, captured in the frame, exhibited a noticeable hesitance in embracing Preetam. It was an unusual sight, as I recalled

Preetam's previous girlfriends being bold and self-assured.

Shyness seemed foreign to his romantic encounters, leaving me pondering the significance of this deviation.

Intrigued by this observation, I continued to peruse the collection of photographs, searching for further clues. To my surprise, in each image, Neelima appeared visibly uncomfortable, her unease palpable.

It was as if something weighed on her, casting a shadow over their interactions.

Questions began to swirl within my mind. What was the reason behind Neelima's hesitance and discomfort? What secrets lay hidden behind their seemingly blissful facade?

The more I delved into the photographs, the deeper my curiosity grew, propelling me to unravel the mystery that shrouded their relationship.

As Preetam emerged from the kitchen, balancing two bowls of noodles and two glasses of orange juice, I found myself caught in a moment of hesitation.

In one hand, I clutched the photo album, and in the other, a printout of an email that held some significance. The timing of his return momentarily caused a delay in my actions, unsure of how to proceed.

Preetam, unaware of my internal conflict, took the letter from my hand and placed one of the glasses in my grasp. The exchange felt slightly awkward, as I had intended to share the contents of the letter with him.

Nevertheless, I resolved to find an opportune moment to broach the subject, determined to uncover the truth that lay within the printed words.

Preetam took notice of my unwillingness to let go of the letter, even as I held the glass of juice. Taking a sip from his own glass, he casually inquired, "What's so important about that letter? You seem quite invested in it."

Silently, a tear escaped from my eyes, landing on the waterproof cover page of the album.

It seemed as though the album itself carried a message, whispering softly, "There are waterproof books, but not tear-proof cheeks." In that moment, the weight of emotion overwhelmed me, each tear carrying its own story.

Preetam, sensing my tears, remained silent, his gaze fixed on the pages of the album. The air between us grew heavy with unspoken words, as the photographs within the album held memories both cherished and bittersweet.

Together, we embarked on a journey through those captured moments, finding solace in the silence that enveloped us. It was written in the letter:

My dearest Anand,

As I sit down to pen these words, my heart feels heavy with the weight of a difficult decision that I must convey to you.

It pains me to say that I can no longer continue our relationship, but the reasons behind this choice are not what you might expect. Allow me to explain.

Recently, I received a devastating phone call that shook the very foundation of my world. It informed me that my father had suffered a stroke and was fighting for his life in the hospital.

Hastening to his side, I witnessed the severity of his condition as he lay on his deathbed, each breath a fragile thread connecting him to this realm.

It was in those final moments that he revealed a long-held secret, one that altered my perception of our reality.

You see, my parents' union was not one embraced by society. It was an inter-caste love marriage, a bond that faced immense opposition from both their families.

Their love was met with hostility and scorn, forcing them to navigate a world intent on tearing them apart.

Tragically, after my birth, my mother fell gravely ill, and her own family turned their backs, refusing to offer her solace in her darkest hours. She suffered in silence, and her pain ultimately claimed her life.

In his final moments, my father made me promise him something profound. He implored me to learn from their experiences and to make choices that would secure a happier future, even if it meant sacrificing present desires.

It is this promise that compels me to end our relationship, as I strive to honor the wishes of the man who loved me unconditionally.

Please understand that this decision weighs heavily on my heart, and it is not a reflection of my feelings for you.

The reality of our world, with its barriers and constraints, has left me questioning whether the stories we witnessed in movies were merely exaggerated fantasies.

Nevertheless, I must follow the path set before me, guided by the love and lessons of my parents.

With a heavy heart, I sign this letter as "Avantika," knowing that my actions may be seen as betrayal. Please remember that it is my duty to fulfill a promise, and in doing so, I hope to create a future that aligns with my father's wishes.

The Betrayer,

Avantika

Preetam's voice trembled with disbelief as he processed the revelation before him.

The realization that Preeti and Avantika were, in fact, the same person hit him with a force greater than the impact of my separation from her. Confusion clouded his expression, his mind struggling to reconcile this unexpected twist in our shared narrative.

"Yes, Preeti and I came from different castes. She was Christian, and I believe her decision to end our relationship stemmed from the fear that our love would face the same opposition as her parents did," I said, retrieving the letter from Preetam's grasp.

Preetam, his voice filled with concern, responded, "How could she think that way, my dear friend? And I don't believe her father meant any harm by his words."

Nodding solemnly, I replied, "I understand, but the weight of fear and the scars of a painful past might have clouded her perception. It seems that the theory you proposed, 'love is a game,' has indeed come to fruition. Look at how my own game has come to an end."

As we sat in contemplative silence, the sound of footsteps echoed through the house, drawing our attention. It didn't take long for us to recognize the newcomer—Neelima.

My heart skipped a beat, and a flurry of questions flooded my mind. Sensing my confusion, Preetam quickly retrieved an envelope, handing it to me with a knowing expression.

The envelope held the answers to the questions that weighed heavy on my heart. With trembling hands, I gingerly opened it, the contents revealing a truth that would irrevocably alter the course of our intertwined lives.

He carefully retrieved some medical reports from the envelope, placing them in my hands. Although my understanding of medical terminology was limited, I tried my best to decipher the information before me.

It became apparent that Preetam was diagnosed with a condition known as Fatal Familial Insomnia.

Curiosity and concern filled my voice as I inquired, "What is this disease, Preetam?"

In a somber tone, he explained, "It's a sleep disorder, my friend. A relentless progression that gradually robs the patient of their ability to sleep, hour by hour, until they are left with an agonizing state of sleeplessness."

Relief washed over me as I absorbed the information. "Oh, Preetam, you really scared me there. I thought it was some grave illness like AIDS or something even more severe," I chuckled nervously, attempting to lighten the mood with a poor attempt at humor.

The room fell into a heavy silence as Preetam and Neelima continued to bear the weight of their circumstances.

Preetam's voice resonated with a mix of sadness and resignation as he shared the harsh reality of his condition. "It's even worse, my friend. Fatal Familial Insomnia has no cure, no treatment," he uttered with a heavy sigh. The gravity of his words hung in the air, leaving a palpable sense of despair.

Preetam continued to recount his recent hardships, explaining how his company had faced a crisis that ultimately led to its closure.

Left with meager resources to sustain himself, he watched as his so-called girlfriends abandoned him, offering only minimal financial support, mere fragments of what he had once invested in them.

However, amidst the desolation, Neelima remained by his side, an unwavering presence of love and support.

A glimmer of hope emerged as Preetam shared his newfound belief in love, albeit in the face of impending tragedy. Time had become an unyielding adversary, with only a dwindling eight months, or possibly even less, left for him to live.

The deterioration of his mental stability loomed on the horizon, foretold by the medical professionals. Yet, Neelima's steadfast commitment defied the odds, her hand held tightly in his, a testament to the enduring power of love.

In that poignant moment, the room was filled with a bittersweet mixture of sorrow and gratitude. Preetam and Neelima had forged a bond that transcended the limitations of time and circumstances.

Together, they would face the uncertain road ahead, finding solace in the love and companionship that would carry them through the darkest moments yet to come.

With tears staining my cheeks, I gathered the strength to step outside, the weight of the situation still heavy on my shoulders. As I got behind the wheel of my car, determination settled within me, propelling me forward on a path of decisive action.

I had resolved to leave my job, to abandon the familiar surroundings that only served as constant reminders of her presence.

Driving through the streets, each passing landmark seemed to mock me with memories of the past. It became clear that a change of scenery was necessary, a chance to create distance between myself and the painful remnants of our shared experiences.

While I understood that this decision was not a true solution, it was the only recourse available to me at that moment.

In that solitary drive, the road ahead held a glimmer of hope. It offered the prospect of healing and finding solace in a place where her memories wouldn't haunt me relentlessly.

Though I knew that escaping the pain wouldn't be easy, I was determined to embark on this journey, believing that time and distance would eventually mend the wounds that still bled within my heart.

Chapter 5

Resignation

The following day, as I made my way to the city to submit my resignation letter, I found myself caught in the familiar congestion of traffic within my town.

Amidst the chaos, my attention was drawn to a woman running aimlessly across the road, her frantic eyes scanning every passing vehicle. As she drew nearer to my car, I recognized her instantly.

It was the same woman to whom I had offered money to feed her child on that fateful party night.

Intrigued by her erratic behavior, I parked my car near the bar where she had purchased the drink. Anxious to uncover the reason behind her distress, I approached the bartender and inquired about her unusual actions.

What I learned next struck me with a profound shock. The bartender revealed that the woman had been deeply attached to her child, but a group from an orphanage had taken the child away in a vehicle.

Since that heart-wrenching day, she had spiraled into a state of madness, desperately searching for her beloved son among the passing vehicles, clinging to a glimmer of hope that she would be reunited with him once more.

The weight of this revelation bore down on me, blending with the heaviness that already burdened my heart. It was a stark reminder of the harsh realities that people faced, the invisible battles that unfolded beneath the surface of our everyday lives.

The world was filled with stories of love, loss, and the relentless pursuit of what was cherished most. In that moment, a renewed sense of empathy washed over me, a reminder that the complexities of life often exceeded our understanding.

As I drove away from the bar, the image of that distraught woman lingered in my thoughts.

Her unwavering love for her child had led her on a desperate quest, a quest that resonated with the longing and anguish I felt within my own heart.

That day had unraveled the intricacies and profound philosophies of life, shattering the theories and beliefs I had constructed based on my own experiences.

It had exposed the fallibility of our judgments and the ever-changing nature of truth. Initially, I believed wholeheartedly in the existence of true love, while Preetam remained skeptical.

However, when Preeti left me, my faith in love was shattered, while Preetam, in his darkest moments, found solace and renewed faith through Neelima's unwavering support.

The encounter with the beggar woman had added to the chaos in my mind, challenging my preconceived notions.

In the midst of these thoughts, I found myself back in my office, preparing my resignation letter. As I focused on the task at hand, my eyes fell upon a letter resting on my desk, capturing my attention.

Curiosity piqued, I reached for it and began to read the words written upon its pages, unaware of the profound impact it would have on my journey.

My beloved Anand,

In the depths of my heart, I am overwhelmed with a flood of emotions, longing to express the remorse that has consumed me. The relationships we come to regret are often the ones we never truly deserved, and I find myself grappling with the weight of this truth.

Oh, how I ache for the time lost, for the misunderstandings that clouded our connection.

As I reflect upon the oath my father took from me, I now understand the profound significance of his words. His intention was for me to forge a path towards a future filled with happiness.

Yet, in my fear and misguided perceptions, I failed to recognize that you are the very essence of my future and the very source of my joy.

The barriers of caste, once seemingly insurmountable, now appear as mere shadows of my own insecurities and madness.

My heart cries out for reconciliation, for a chance to rebuild what we have lost.

Every moment without you has been a torment, a relentless reminder of the depth of my love for you.

I am haunted by the memories we shared, and the realization that I pushed you away out of fear and ignorance pierces my soul.

Oh, my beloved, please believe in the sincerity of my words. I yearn to reclaim the love we once held, to defy the odds and chart a course towards a future where our hearts beat as one.

May our souls intertwine once more, weaving a tapestry of love and redemption that surpasses the boundaries of society!

With a love that knows no bounds,

Avantika/Preeti

I turned around, and there she stood, a vision before my eyes. Overwhelmed with a mix of emotions, I couldn't resist the impulse that surged through me—I embraced her tightly.

In that moment, it seemed as though the world around us faded away, and it was just the two of us, entwined in a long-awaited reunion.

Surprisingly, nobody seemed to bat an eye, as if the gravity of our connection had erased any doubts or judgments.

As the embrace gradually loosened, a longing to understand her actions welled up within me. With a hint of pain in my voice, I mustered the courage to ask the question that had plagued my thoughts, "Why did you hurt me so deeply, without a single apology?"

Her response, both simple and profound, pierced through the silence, "Because I am a girl." Her words hung in the air, bearing the weight of unspoken complexities and societal expectations.

Amidst the bittersweet atmosphere, a beep from my phone disrupted the moment. I glanced down, discovering a notification that read "Avantika is online."

A surge of anticipation washed over me, a glimmer of hope that our online encounter would open the door to a deeper understanding, a chance to heal the wounds of the past and forge a new path forward.

Chapter 6

The Miracles of Love

As the sun began to set, casting a warm, golden glow over the world, destiny unfolded its final act in the lives of Preetam and Neelima.

The weight of their journey and the fragility of their time together hung heavy in the air, leaving us yearning for a miracle to bridge the gap between their intertwined destinies.

With bated breath, we stood witness to the extraordinary power of love, yearning for a resolution that would leave an indelible mark on our souls. And then, in the midst of the gathering dusk, the unimaginable occurred.

Preetam, frail and vulnerable, yet filled with an unwavering spirit, took Neelima's trembling hand in his own.

As they stood together, a surge of hope emanated from their entwined fingers, rippling through their bodies and igniting a flame of vitality within.

In that extraordinary moment, time seemed to stand still. Preetam's weakened form straightened, his eyes shining with an otherworldly radiance.

Neelima, her gaze filled with a mixture of awe and disbelief, witnessed a transformation unfolding before her very eyes.

Miraculously, the ravages of illness began to recede, as if time itself were rewinding.

Preetam's strength returned, his vitality renewed, as if the universe had conspired to grant him a precious gift – a chance to embrace the life he had been destined to live.

As our hearts swelled with a mixture of disbelief and joy, we watched in awe as Preetam and Neelima embarked on a new chapter, their destinies united against all odds.

Their love, once tested by the trials of mortality, now defied the limitations of the physical world.

Together, they forged ahead, hand in hand, their love radiating like a beacon of hope for all those who had witnessed their extraordinary journey.

The chapters of their lives unfolded with newfound purpose, each step forward a testament to the resilience of the human spirit and the boundless miracles that love can bring.

As we parted ways, forever impacted by the miracles we had witnessed, we carried with us the profound understanding that love, in its purest form, possesses a transformative power that transcends the boundaries of reason and logic.

In the years that followed, the story of Preetam and Neelima would become the stuff of legends, whispered among kindred spirits seeking solace and inspiration.

Their love story, forever etched in the annals of time, served as a reminder that in the realm of love, anything is possible – even the most extraordinary miracles.

And so, dear reader, as we bid farewell to these cherished characters, forever united in the embrace of their extraordinary love, let us carry their story within our hearts.

May it serve as a reminder that the power of love knows no bounds, that miracles can unfold when we dare to believe in the impossible!

For in the grand tapestry of life, it is the stories of love, hope, and resilience that endure, forever etching their mark on the souls of those who are fortunate enough to bear witness.

The end.

Milton Keynes UK
Ingram Content Group UK Ltd.
UKHW040759010823
426141UK00001B/164